School Scare

With special thanks to Jim Collins

First published in Great Britain in 2012 by Buster Books,
an imprint of Michael O'Mara Books Limited,
9 Lion Yard, Tremadoc Road, London SW4 7NQ

www.busterbooks.co.uk
www.monstrousmaud.co.uk

Series created by Working Partners Limited
Text copyright © Working Partners Limited 2012

Cover design by Nicola Theobald

Illustration copyright © Buster Books 2012
Illustrations by Sarah Horne

HOUSE OF HORROR™ copyright © House Industries

A CIP catalogue record for this book is available
from the British Library.

ISBN: 978–1–78055–075–6 in paperback print format
ISBN: 978–1–78055–087–9 in Epub format
ISBN: 978–1–78055–086–2 in Mobipocket format

1 3 5 7 9 10 8 6 4 2

Papers used by Michael O'Mara Books are natural,
recyclable products made from wood grown in sustainable forests.
The manufacturing processes conform to the environmental
regulations of the country of origin.

Printed and bound in July 2012 by CPI Group (UK) Ltd,
108 Beddington Lane, Croydon, CR0 4YY, United Kingdom

School
Scare

A. B. Saddlewick

BUSTER

Chapter One

Maud Montague's pet rat had escaped again. "No, Quentin!" she hissed.

Her rat was scuttling along the top of the back seat of the school bus, heading straight for Warren, the werewolf from the year above. Warren had his head back, snoozing, with his tongue lolling from one side of his mouth.

"Quentin, come back right now!" called out Maud, as loudly as she dared.

Quentin turned back to her, brushing the wolf's stubby black nose with his tail as he did so.

"RaCHOO!" Warren woke up with a noise that was part sneeze, part roar.

Quentin squeaked and launched himself off Warren's shoulder and into Maud's pocket.

"Grrroar! What did you wake me up for?" Warren asked Billy Bones, the skeleton who was sitting next to him.

"It wasn't me," said Billy.

"Well, why are you grinning then?" asked Warren.

"I can't stop," said Billy. "Skeletons always grin."

Warren snarled. "How convenient."

The brakes screeched, throwing everyone out of their seats, and the bus skidded to a halt at the side of the road. The driver honked the horn in three long blasts. Maud picked herself off the floor, checked Quentin was okay, and peered through the dirty windows. A limousine with the number plate W1CK3D zoomed past. Who on earth could be in such a hurry?

"Has anyone seen my left arm?" said Zombie Zak.

"It's here," said the driver, fishing under the pedals.

The bus spluttered back into life and jolted away again.

"I wonder who that was," Maud muttered.

When they reached the school, Maud was shocked to see the big black car parked in front. Surely none of her teachers could afford a vehicle like that?

One of the back doors opened, revealing an interior of spotless cream leather. A girl wearing buckled shoes and a ragged black dress emerged. Maud couldn't believe it. It was her classmate Poisonous Penelope!

Penelope was a witch with a pointed hat and purple hair who usually took the bus with everyone else. What was she doing in such a fancy car?

"See you later," said Penelope to the driver.

Maud couldn't see his face under the brim of his hat, but his hand emerged from the window to wave goodbye, and Maud noticed a large gold ring on his index finger.

Penelope slammed the door and the car turned around and tore off down the driveway, throwing tiny chips of gravel into the air. A group of younger pupils scattered, getting out of the way just in time.

Maud ran up to Penelope as she climbed the school's stone steps.

"That's a fancy car, isn't it?" asked Maud. "You didn't cast a spell on the lottery numbers, did you?"

"It's my uncle Peregrine's car," said Penelope, sneering at Maud. "Well, *one* of his cars."

"How many does he have?" asked Maud.

"Enough to fill the humongous driveway of his ginormous house," said Penelope. "I'm staying with him while my parents are on holiday in Salem. So I won't have to go on that smelly bus again for a couple of weeks."

"It's only smelly when Zombie Zak forgets his after-grave spray," said Maud. "I don't know why you're being so snooty."

"Because Uncle Peregrine owns hundreds of hotels and has pots of cash," said Penelope as she strode through the school's arched doorway. "But I wouldn't expect a scruffbag like you to understand."

Maud hung back in the entrance hall as a crowd of admirers gathered around the witch. Penelope was hard work at the best of times. This was going to make her totally impossible.

"Gather round, my little monsters," said Professor Gool.

The science teacher smoothed down the twin tufts of white hair on his head, but they sprang right back up again. He fished a notebook out of his lab coat and beckoned the pupils around the desk at the front of the classroom.

"You too, Montague," he said.

Maud was peering out of the narrow window to see if she could spot her vampire best friend, Paprika. He often flew to school in bat form, but he was late today. Maud was surprised. He'd been really looking forward to this lesson on bringing the dead back to life.

Maud walked over to the front desk and stood next to Wilf. He was a werewolf, Warren's younger brother, and her second best friend. Professor Gool whipped a sheet away to reveal a pair of metal clips wired to a generator.

"Wow! Monstrous!" said Wilf.

"Me first," said Frank Stein, a hulking pupil with green skin and metal bolts sticking out of his neck. "It's just like the one we have at home."

"I'm afraid not," said Professor Gool. "I really can't demonstrate this on pupils anymore. Health and safety regulations."

All the students groaned.

"It's not my decision," said the teacher. "If it was up to me, you could run electricity through yourselves until your little eyeballs sizzled and popped out. It certainly did me no harm when I was your age."

"You'd better demonstrate on a dead frog then," said Penelope. "I've got a couple in my lunch box for spells."

"I can't even do that anymore," said Professor Gool. "Animal rights."

Penelope rolled her eyes.

"I'm going to have to demonstrate on this," he said, dragging a suit of armour out from under the desk. "It doesn't have any feelings." He held up the electrode clips. "Now, who can tell me where these go?"

Frank Stein pointed to the bolts on either side of his neck.

"That's right," said Professor Gool.

He attached the electrodes to either side of

the helmet and turned the generator up a notch. It started to rattle up and down.

"Now," said Professor Gool. "Watch what happens as I increase the power."

He turned the dial, and the generator gave out a high-pitched whistle. The armour shook violently.

On the other side of the classroom, Maud noticed that Penelope was wiggling her fingers and muttering under her breath.

"Sir, Penelope's casting a spell," said Maud.

"Shush," said the teacher. "I'm trying to concentrate."

Professor Gool was focusing on the dial and didn't see the electrodes unhook themselves from the helmet and float down magically towards Wilf's hairy paws.

"Now we increase the power further," said the teacher, cranking up the dial.

"Owwwwwwwww! Hoooooooooooooowl!" Wilf sprang into the air, and his fur stood on end as the clips touched his paws.

Professor Gool stared at the lifeless suit of armour. "Oh dear, that didn't work. I'll try a bit more."

"Wait, Sir!" said Maud.

Professor Gool yanked the dial up again. Wilf yelped as if his tail was trapped in a car door. Smoke billowed out of his ears, and the classroom started to smell faintly like a barbecue.

"SIR!" shouted Maud.

Finally, the teacher noticed the frizzling werewolf and shut the power off.

Penelope burst into a loud cackle, while everyone else crowded around Wilf anxiously.

"I'm fine," said Wilf, though his hair was still standing on end, making him look like a giant, fluffy teddy.

"Let's try again," said Professor Gool. "And this time, cut out the silly pranks."

Maud frowned at Penelope, then checked the

window again. There was no sign of Paprika, but she did notice a blue car pulling up in the driveway. Very strange. The only vehicles Maud had ever seen in the car park were the spluttering school bus and the battered old cars the teachers drove. This looked like a perfectly normal car.

A young woman stepped out of the car and pressed a button on her key ring that made the car beep. She was wearing a neat grey suit with flat black shoes, and her brown hair was parted at the side. Unless she had a pair of wings or an extra head tucked somewhere, she looked a lot like an ordinary human. But what would a human be doing at a school for monsters?

Professor Gool had just finished hooking up the electrodes again when the school's headmistress floated in through the door. The Head was a ghost with large round glasses and her hair tied back in a bun. She was also Maud's great-aunt Ethel – although the other pupils didn't know that.

The Head usually had a calm, stern expression, but today her eyes were wide, her hands were trembling, and she was floating even further off the ground than usual.

"Clear everything away," the Head shouted. She pointed at the suit of armour. "Cover that thing up."

"What in Hades is the matter?" asked Professor Gool.

"There's an inspector here," she said. "A human inspector. If she works out what kind of school this is, we'll be shut down."

Professor Gool gasped and threw the sheet back over the suit of armour.

The Head pointed at Maud. "Montague! Go downstairs and introduce yourself to the Inspector as Head Girl!"

"I didn't know I was Head Girl," said Maud.

"Well, you are now," said the Head. "If anyone around here can pass for normal, it's you."

"Yes," muttered Penelope. "I wonder why that is?"

Maud blushed. She was the only human pupil at Rotwood, and only a few trusted people knew her secret. But Penelope had recently visited her house and was getting suspicious.

"As for the rest of you," shouted the Head, "put on your disguises, quickly! And don't do anything freaky when the Inspector's here. That means no casting spells, no roaring, and absolutely no removing of limbs."

"Miss!" said Billy Bones, sticking his hand up. "I forgot my disguise today. I didn't know I needed it."

"How many times must I tell you not to leave home without it?" said the Head. She glared at Billy's bare white frame and shook her head. "You'd better hide in the cupboard."

Billy got up and skulked towards the cupboard.

"Miss, I've forgotten mine as well," said Invisible Isabel from the back of the class.

"Well, never mind," said the Head. "Somehow I don't think it will be a problem."

"That's so unfair," said Billy Bones.

"Into the cupboard!" screamed the Head, hovering ever higher in the air. Several pupils flinched with fright. Maud had never seen the Head so panicked before. Billy hurried to obey.

"Right," said the Head, floating back down. "Now, you're all pretending to be humans, remember? We can get through this."

Maud wasn't so sure.

Chapter Two

Maud darted down the torch-lit spiral staircase so fast she made herself dizzy. At the bottom, she turned into Rotwood's huge, dusty entrance hall. The Inspector had already ventured inside and was peering into the gloom.

"Hello?" she said. "Is anyone there?"

"Hi," said Maud, trying to sound as cheerful as she could. "I'm Maud Montague. I'm the Head Girl of Rotwood. Sorry for the delay. We weren't really expecting you."

"I don't know why not," said the Inspector. "I sent a letter."

She wiped one of the walls with her finger and scowled at the dust collected on it. "Let's get on, shall we?" she said, making a note on her clipboard. "I've got another school to see this afternoon."

"Let me show you around," said Maud. "This is the entrance hall. At break you'll find this area teeming with pupils enthusiastically discussing their homework."

"Where are the lights?" asked the Inspector. "I can hardly judge the cleanliness of your school if I can't see it." She made another note on her clipboard.

Mr Quasimodo lolloped down the entrance hall towards them, carrying a mop and bucket of dark green water. He was hunched forward, but looked up and growled as he approached.

"This is the caretaker," said Maud. "He's got a bit of a bad back at the moment." She turned to Mr Quasimodo and pointed at the ceiling. "I expect you're about to clean away all those cobwebs, aren't you?"

"Cobwebs good," he replied. "Give place atmosphere."

Maud laughed as if this was a joke, and the caretaker grunted and hobbled away. The Inspector made yet another note.

"These doors lead to the classrooms," said Maud, as they continued towards the back of the hall. She didn't really know where the dingy doorways at the sides of the entrance hall went, and she hoped the Inspector wouldn't ask to see inside them. She'd heard the detention dungeon was down there somewhere.

"What are these?" asked the Inspector. She pointed to the cabinet where the school's trophies for Monsterball and Swamp Swimming were stored, as well as the certificates for 'Most Frightening Pupil' and 'Mr Quasimodo's

Special Award for the Ugliest Pupil'.

"It's the old Halloween display," said Maud, desperately scanning around for something normal to show the Inspector. She spotted a red fire extinguisher that looked fairly new. "Over here is our fire safety equipment."

A bat flapped into the entrance hall, on a collision course with the Inspector. Maud frowned and shooed it away while the woman's back was turned. Paprika had certainly picked a bad moment to show up.

"Why does this say 'not to be used on demons or shapeshifters'?" asked the woman, who was crouching down to examine the fire extinguisher.

"They all say that these days," said Maud. "Health and safety."

The Inspector noted this on her clipboard. "I think I'll speak to your headmistress now."

The Head leapt through the wall behind the Inspector and frantically shook her head.

"I'm afraid she's in a meeting," said Maud, thinking fast.

"But my letter said I'd be arriving today," said the Inspector, flipping over the page on her clipboard.

"It's an emergency meeting," said Maud. This wasn't going well. "I could show you up to my classroom if you'd like."

The Inspector tutted. "Very well."

Maud ushered the Inspector over to the spiral staircase at the side of the hall. Most of the torches had blown out, probably because Paprika had flown past so quickly.

"Don't you find it a little dark?" asked the Inspector.

"You get used to it," said Maud, as she took one of the few lit torches down from the wall. She held it up to light the way ahead.

"They let you carry naked flames?" asked the Inspector, lifting her pen.

"Only me," said Maud. "Since I'm Head Girl."

Maud led the way up the stairs. When they reached the classroom, she stopped outside and coughed noisily to give everyone a quick warning.

When she opened the door, she was relieved to see all her classmates sitting calmly behind their desks, their bulky hats and scarves covering their faces. Paprika had even managed to transform and settle behind his desk in time.

Professor Gool was holding a biology textbook in front of him. Maud noticed that he'd written "The anatomy of the living dead" on the blackboard behind him. She edged over as the Inspector was looking around and erased the word 'living'.

"The central nervous system consists of the brain and the spinal cord," said Professor Gool.

The pupils dutifully wrote down the words

he was reading. The cupboard at the back of the classroom began to rattle, and the Inspector spun around. "I think someone might be in there," she said, striding over to it.

Oh no! Billy Bones, thought Maud.

"I expect it's just the wind," Maud said, following at her heels.

The Inspector threw open the cupboard door. Maud winced. Without his disguise, it was clear Billy was a skeleton, not a human. The whole class gasped.

It's all over, Maud thought miserably.

Billy stood perfectly still as Professor Gool walked over and pointed at his skull. "You see? The central nervous system runs down from the skull, seen here, to the backbone."

The moment the Inspector looked down at her clipboard, Billy lifted his thumb bone to his nose hole and waggled his fingers up and down. A few pupils tittered, and the Inspector looked up. Billy flopped his arm back down again.

"Let me show you the hall," said Maud, leading the Inspector out of the room. Billy waved behind her back, which caused the class to giggle once more.

"They seem in very high spirits today," said the Inspector.

"Yes," said Maud. "We do love biology lessons!"

At the bottom of the stairs, Maud led the Inspector down a narrow passageway to the assembly hall, a cavernous vault with ancient stone pillars and ornate wall carvings.

Mr Fortissimo the music teacher was playing the organ at the far end of the hall, arching his back and jerking from side to side as he slammed his fingers down on the keys. Maud was glad he was facing away from the Inspector, so she couldn't see his monstrous face.

As Mr Fortissimo played, Miss Maria Callous, the choir mistress, was leading her class in a rendition of "Mourning Has Broken". She had bright green hair and a string of squidgy eyeballs around her neck, but Maud thought those could pass for really big pearls from a distance.

Mine is the darkness, mine is the mourning, sang the class. Thankfully, the siren sisters from class 4C almost drowned out the werewolves.

"A little bit howly, aren't they?" said the Inspector.

"And this door takes us back to the entrance hall," said Maud hurriedly, leading her away down another shadowy corridor.

The Inspector peered through her notes. "So, do you enjoy coming to this school?"

"Absolutely," said Maud, as they emerged back in the entrance hall. "I think it's the best school in the country."

The Inspector noted this down and said,

"Well, then everything seems to be in order."

Maud stared. "You mean we've passed?"

"Yes," said the Inspector. "There are a couple of cosmetic issues I'll mention in my report, such as the dust and poor lighting. But on the whole, it seems as though the pupils are learning a great deal."

"Monstrous," said Maud, shaking the Inspector's hand. "I mean, wonderful."

"I'll be in touch if I have any other questions," added the Inspector.

✶ ★ ✳ ☆ ★ ✳

Maud watched as the woman made her way down the stone steps outside the school. As soon as the Inspector was gone, the Head popped through the back wall.

"Well done, Maud," she said. "Now, you'd better get back to your lesson."

Maud leapt back up the stairs two at a time.

"She's gone!" she said, as she threw open the classroom door.

"I don't think I could have taken any more of that rubbish," said Professor Gool, tossing the biology textbook into the bin.

"Right, let's get back to the proper lesson."

He pulled the sheet off the suit of armour and flicked the generator back on. As the pupils peeled off scarves and coats, Billy Bones stepped out of the cupboard, cracking his knuckles.

"Gather round then," said Professor Gool. "Observe the effects of a full power dose of electricity on the specimen."

Professor Gool cranked up the generator, and the suit of armour sat upright on the desk. The teacher turned the power down again, and it flopped back down with a clatter.

"Sir, what happens if you turn it up to where it says DANGER?" asked Penelope, pointing at the dial.

"We can't show you that," said the Professor.

"I understand," said Penelope, sighing dramatically. "Health and safety rules must be more important than our education."

Professor Gool glanced over his shoulder. "Well, I don't suppose a quick blast could hurt."

He cranked the dial all the way to maximum, and the suit of armour sat upright again. This time it yanked the electrodes out of its neck and jumped down off the table.

"Get back on that table this instant!" shouted Professor Gool. "I shan't warn you again."

The suit of armour ran over to the other side of the classroom and danced around one of the desks, shaking its arms up and down defiantly.

"Come back! Now!" shouted Professor Gool.

The suit of armour danced so vigorously that the helmet fell off its neck and clanked to the floor. Its headless body flailed around the room with arms outstretched, knocking bags and books off desks.

"I know who that reminds me of," said

Penelope. She ran over to Oscar and snatched his head off. She held it out of his reach, while his body jumped up to grab it.

"Hey!" said Maud protectively. Oscar was very proud that he could take his own head off whenever he wanted, but that didn't mean Penelope could snatch it off like that.

"Sir, Penelope's got my head," said Oscar's head.

"Penelope! Give that back immediately!" said Professor Gool. He ran after the suit of armour, which was still clanking around the classroom. "You know it's against school rules to remove other pupils' body parts without their permission."

Penelope threw Oscar's head to Billy Bones, who caught it and clambered on to the desk at the front.

Maud was rushing over to help Oscar, when she heard the door creak. She turned to see the Inspector standing in the doorway. "Sorry, I forgot to ask …" Her mouth dropped open.

"Uh-oh," said Oscar's head.

"I can explain," said Maud.

The Inspector screamed, spun around, and ran out of the door.

"It's not what you think!" shouted Maud. She sprinted into the corridor and saw the Inspector disappearing down the stairwell. "We were just trying on our Halloween costumes!"

The screams of the Inspector echoed through the stairwell as Maud chased after her. By the time Maud got to the entrance hall, the Inspector had already reached the front door.

"Please don't go!" shouted Maud, one last time.

But the Inspector flung open the door and scrambled down the stone steps outside.

She lost a shoe, and hobbled towards her car, scrabbling in her handbag for her keys. She'd almost reached it, when a stag beetle the size of a horse came charging towards her.

"Help!" shrieked the Inspector.

She screamed even louder than before and hopped away from the lumbering insect.

Mr Galahad, the PE teacher, came running around the corner, twirling a rope in his hands.

"Don't run away, woman," he yelled, huffing. "Stand your ground. Bessie can smell fear!"

He threw a lasso over the beetle's neck just as it lunged at the Inspector with its antlers.

The Inspector yanked open her car door and leapt inside. She sped away, her tyres screeching.

"She seemed jolly uptight," Mr Galahad said as he led the stag beetle away. "Was she anyone important?"

"Yes," sighed Maud. "I'm afraid she was."

Chapter Three

*M*aud couldn't stop thinking about the disastrous inspection as she opened a bag of crisps that evening. Quentin jumped out of her pocket and ran down her arm towards the crisps.

"Wait, Quentin!" said Maud. "Not until I offer them."

Quentin paused on Maud's sleeve and looked back and forth from her to the crisps.

"That's better," said Maud. She handed him a crisp, and he held it in both paws as he gnawed on it.

"I hope the school doesn't get in too much trouble," said Maud.

Her twin sister Milly stomped into the living room and dumped herself down on the sofa next to her. She was still wearing her neat navy-blue Primrose Towers uniform.

"Well, that was a yawnsome day," said Milly. "Our class spent the whole morning making sure all the pencils were the same length in time for our inspection, and guess what? The Inspector didn't even turn up."

Maud suspected the poor Inspector had needed a long rest after her experience at Rotwood.

Mr Montague walked in and crashed down on his chair without even taking his driving gloves off.

"Busy day at the garage?" asked Maud.

"That would be putting it mildly," said Mr Montague. "You'll never guess who we've just won as a client. Only Peregrine Prenderghast!"

"Never heard of him," said Milly. "Is he on TV?"

"As a matter of fact, he is. He's in those adverts for his hotel chain. You must have heard of Prenderghast Hotels. 'Have a magical stay', and all that."

"What does he want with you?" asked Maud.

"He's asked us to service his entire fleet of black limousines. It's quite an honour to be chosen, really. If you think those machines are beautiful on the outside, wait until you see their engines."

"Monstrous," said Maud, though she really thought all car engines looked the same. As her dad continued to waffle about engines, Maud remembered the car that Penelope had flounced out of that morning. Wasn't that a black limousine? And hadn't she mentioned something about her uncle owning hotels?

When she walked into the assembly hall the following morning, Maud looked around for Penelope, so she could ask her about her uncle. But Penelope wasn't there. Instead, Maud settled down next to Paprika and Wilf, as Mr Fortissimo played a sad tune on the organ.

The Head floated through the wall, lifted up her hand to stop Mr Fortissimo, and peered at the pupils through her large round glasses. "As you might have gathered, the inspection yesterday was not a success. Sadly, the Inspector's report claimed that the school was full of headless creatures, walking skeletons and giant insects."

Mr Fortissimo held his monstrous head in his hands.

"Fortunately for us," continued the Head, "the Inspector in question has now been temporarily admitted into Spooglewood Home for the Deranged."

Several of the pupils cheered at this, but

Maud didn't join in. She felt sorry for the poor Inspector.

"Unfortunately," said the Head, "this means that the school is to be inspected again next week."

The pupils groaned.

"We don't know exactly when the inspection is happening, so we need to make sure this place is as spotless as a human school at all times. That means we need painted walls, polished floors and as many pictures of flowers, bunnies and rainbows as we can handle."

Some of the younger monsters gasped. Fluffy animals were as frightening to them as vampires and zombies would be to humans.

Maud put up her hand.

"Yes, Montague?" said the Head.

"What will happen if we fail?"

The Head's head drooped. "Then I'm afraid Rotwood will be shut down," she said quietly.

Penelope wandered into the hushed hall.

"Sorry I'm late, everyone," she announced. "My limo broke down on the way here. Did I miss anything?"

"Quiet, Penelope," said the Head. "I'm sure your friends will fill you in."

As Maud left the hall, she noticed that Penelope was waiting in the corridor and handing out black envelopes to everyone as they passed.

Paprika got an envelope. Billy got an envelope. Wilf got an envelope. But as Maud approached, Penelope folded her arms.

"You're not invited," she said, glancing scornfully at Maud.

"I didn't want to come anyway," said Maud. "Whatever it is."

Maud jogged through the throng of pupils to catch up with Wilf as he opened his envelope.

"Can I see?" asked Maud.

Wilf showed her a black card with gold lettering.

You are cordially invited to
Penelope Prenderghast's Party
on Saturday.

"That party is going to be rubbish," said Paprika. "Penelope's so horrible that no one will want to go."

"Yeah," said Wilf. "It was really mean of her to electrocute me yesterday. But I might go to the party anyway. If it's half as monstrous as the invitation, it might be worth it."

Maud took the clothes peg from Quentin's paws and gave him a cheese snack as a reward.

"Well done," said Maud. "Clever boy!"

She'd spent all Saturday morning in the kitchen training him to fetch things, and he'd been doing brilliantly. She knew he was very clever, but even she was surprised at how quickly he was getting the hang of it. Sometimes he misheard and brought a doormat instead of a placemat, or loo-paper instead of newspaper, but Maud was sure he just needed more practice.

Maud clasped the bag of snacks shut and drew it back. "Next, I want you to fetch me a sock. Do you understand?"

Quentin nodded and ran out of the door.

"Ewww," screamed Milly from the hallway. She burst into the kitchen and stuck her hands on her hips. She was wearing her blue duffel coat with all the toggles neatly done up.

"Mum said you had to stay in the garage if you wanted to play with Quentin at weekends."

"He's not harming anyone," said Maud.

"That's not the point," said Milly. "Imagine if one of our neighbours popped round. This isn't a sewer."

"Our neighbours never pop round," said Maud. "Why have you got your coat on?"

"Mum's driving me to the shops," said Milly. "We've got to create a perfume out of natural ingredients for our school project."

Maud winced. This sounded like exactly the sort of girly project they'd be given at Primrose Towers. Maud was so glad she didn't have to go there anymore.

"I don't suppose you've heard of perfume," said Milly. "Though it might help you cover the smell of that mangy rodent."

Quentin scurried back in. He was dragging Maud's alarm clock in his paws.

"I said 'sock', not 'clock'," said Maud. She sighed. "But that's close enough for a treat."

Maud opened the packet again, and Quentin did a little excited dance.

"Bye, vermin," called Milly. "Oh, and bye Quentin, too." She was giggling to herself as she slammed the door.

"Thank goodness she's gone," Maud said to Quentin. She hated going with Milly and her mum on their dreary shopping trips. Last time they'd gone to the shopping centre, Quentin had panicked and run through some changing rooms, causing five women to run out screaming with just their bras and knickers on.

"Now let's try again," said Maud. "Fetch me a sock. S-O-C-K."

As Quentin hurried away, Maud heard her dad taking a call in the garage. "But I need to be here to look after my daughter …"

A few seconds later, Maud's dad rushed into the kitchen and squirted washing-up liquid on his greasy hands. "Sorry," he said. "Work emergency. You'll have to come along."

"Come along where?" asked Maud.

"To Peregrine Prenderghast's mansion," said Mr Montague. "He's just summoned me to fix one of his cars. I told him it was Saturday, my day off, but he said that meant I could get there quicker. He's not the sort of person you can argue with."

Maud was beginning to see where Penelope got her charming personality from.

Quentin ran back into the kitchen with a crumpled white sock clasped in his mouth.

"Well done!" said Maud. "But you'll have to eat your reward in the car."

She handed Quentin the snack, scooped him into her pocket and ran out of the front door.

They zoomed out of the driveway. Every time her dad stopped at a red light, he looked up at it and tapped his fingers on the steering wheel as if that would make it change quicker. They sped out of town through housing estates, then into a landscape of open fields. After half an hour, they came to a pair of wide black gates containing the initials 'PP' shaped from iron.

Mr Montague waved to a security camera on top of the gates, and they opened soundlessly.

Mr Prenderghast's driveway was longer than Maud's street. At the bottom, a wide grey building with three floors of gleaming windows loomed. In front, Maud saw an elaborate fountain spurting around a bronze statue of a man with no shirt on. As she passed the figure, Maud noticed something strange about it. Although it had the strong body of a Greek god, it had thinning hair, a low forehead and small, piggy eyes.

Finally, her dad pulled into a narrow gap between the black limousines that lined the driveway. They were all spotlessly clean and had strange number plates, such as D3MON, D3V1L and SP3LL.

As they got out of the car, the thick wooden door to Mr Prenderghast's mansion opened. Out stepped a man with a long, pale face, wearing a smart black jacket and a top hat.

"Good afternoon," said the doorman. "I am Igor. Please step inside."

As Maud walked past him, she noticed he was wearing a gold ring on his index finger.

He had to be the driver who'd been bringing Penelope to school.

Igor led them down a long hallway lined with oil paintings. Each one showed the man with the tiny eyes from the statue Maud had seen in the driveway. In the paintings, he was wrestling lions on African plains, driving flags into snow-capped mountain peaks, and posing with winning football teams.

Although the house looked as though it was two hundred years old, it seemed to be fitted with amazing technology. The chandeliers above them lit and then blew themselves out as they passed, and the door at the end of the corridor swung open as they approached.

Inside was a room with dark red wallpaper, lit by elaborate candelabras. The man from the paintings was hunched forward in a green leather armchair in the centre of the room. He wore a purple smoking jacket.

"Allow me to introduce Mr Peregrine

Prenderghast," said Igor.

"You can call me Peregrine Prenderghast the Third for short," said the man in the chair, a smirk spreading over his lips. Maud wondered where she'd seen that smirk before and then she realised it was the grin that appeared on Penelope's face whenever she did something especially spiteful.

"I'm Maurice Montague," said Maud's dad, holding out his hand.

"Mr Prenderghast does not shake hands," hissed Igor. "They're filthy with germs."

"I'm sorry," said Mr Montague.

Maud didn't know why her dad was apologising. She thought it was Prenderghast who should be ashamed. She really thought Prender*ghastly* was a better name for him.

Mr Prenderghast clicked his fingers, and the candles in the room dimmed. "Now Montague, I've got a problem with one of my cars and I need you to work fast. Do you understand?"

"Of course," said Maud's dad. "Just point out the car in question and I'll roll my sleeves up."

"Very well," said Mr Prenderghast. "Perhaps your child should go and play with my niece Penelope. She's in the middle of her homework, but I'm sure she won't mind."

"I think I will," said Maud, staring right at him. She didn't like the way he was talking about her as if she wasn't there.

"That's of no consequence," snapped Mr Prenderghast. "Upstairs, turn left, third door on the right. Oh, and just one more thing ..."

"Yes?" asked Maud.

"Have a magical stay," said Mr Prenderghast, his slimy smile returning.

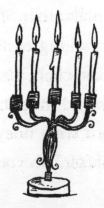

Chapter Four

Candles flickered on and off as Maud wandered down the corridor looking for Penelope's room. It certainly seemed odd that Penelope should be getting on with her homework on a Saturday afternoon. Usually she did it on the school bus, or cast a spell on someone else to make them do it for her.

Maud counted along to the third doorway on the right and knocked. There was no answer, so she creaked the door open. The room inside looked more like a laboratory than a bedroom. There was a bank of TV screens across the far wall, and in the middle was a metal table with a sheet covering a lumpy shape.

"What are you doing?" boomed a voice from behind Maud.

Maud turned around. Igor was staring at her. His pale skin was now flushing red, and he was pointing at the open door.

"Sorry," said Maud. "I was looking for Penelope."

"Mr Prenderghast gave you clear instructions to go to the top floor," said Igor. "This is his private study, which no one, I repeat NO ONE, is allowed into. Do you understand?"

"Yes," said Maud. She darted out of the room, and Igor locked the door behind her. What was hidden under the sheet? A body, maybe? Maud shuddered as Igor led her up a flight of polished wooden steps to a door with 'Penelope's Hovel' scrawled inside the silhouette of a black cat.

Igor waited and watched as Maud knocked.

"Come in!" said a voice.

Maud opened the door. Penelope was stirring a large cauldron with a wooden ladle and examining something that looked like a recipe book. She looked up at Maud. "Oh, no. What on earth are you doing here?"

"My dad's visiting your uncle," said Maud.

This only seemed to confuse Penelope further. "But Uncle Peri is friends with Russian billionaires, hip-hop superstars and professional footballers. What would he want with your father?"

"He's come to fix a car," said Maud.

"Oh, I see," said Penelope. "Like a servant. That makes sense."

She turned back to her book and continued stirring her potion.

"What are you making?" asked Maud.

"Invisibility potion," said Penelope. "It's from this new spell book my uncle gave me. It's miles more advanced than the ones we've got at school, so I won't try and explain it to you."

"Make something disappear, then," said Maud.

"It's not quite ready yet," said Penelope. "I think it needs a few more caterpillar eyeballs."

Penelope grabbed something that looked like a pepper mill from her desk and ground it into the cauldron.

Maud walked across the big black bedroom to the large window at the back of Penelope's room. It looked out over the grounds behind the house, which were even grander than the driveway at the front. Neat gravel paths spread out across a flat lawn that went on for miles, broken up by oak trees shading wooden benches and tables. A stone bridge crossed a brook on the left, and there was a maze of high privet hedges on the right.

"That garden looks amazing," said Maud. "Can we go outside?"

Penelope stared over at the window, her smug grin slipping. "Uncle Peri doesn't like me running around the grounds. He says I'll mark the grass. I don't mind, though. I'd rather stay in here and work on my potions. Talking of which …"

Penelope picked up a mug from her desk and dipped it in the potion. When she held it up again, the mug faded to nothing in front of Maud's eyes.

"Monstrous!" said Maud. She tapped her jacket pocket. "You've got to see this, Quentin!"

Quentin jumped out of Maud's pocket and darted across the floor.

Penelope shrieked and leapt into the air, spilling the invisibility potion all over her desk.

"Oh no," said Maud, rushing over to pick Quentin up. "I'm sorry. I didn't mean to scare you."

"I wasn't scared!" said Penelope. "Just shocked, that's all."

As Maud scooped up her pet, she saw that the dark top of the desk had disappeared. She caught sight of a letter inside the drawer below:

Dear Head of Rotwood School,

We at the School Inspectorate look forward to visiting your premises on ...

Penelope swiped a wad of tissues across the desk before Maud could read any more. The tissues turned invisible as they soaked up the liquid, and the desk became solid again.

"What was that letter ...?"

Igor entered again. "Your father is leaving now, Miss Montague."

"Already?" asked Maud. She wanted to question Penelope further, but Igor was tapping his foot. "See you on Monday," she said.

"Unfortunately," said Penelope.

Maud followed the doorman down to the

hallway. As she wandered past marble and bronze busts of Mr Prenderghast's piggy face, she wondered about the letter. Could Penelope have stolen it? It would certainly explain why the Head knew nothing about the inspection.

As Maud stepped out into the driveway, Mr Montague carefully lowered the bonnet of a limousine and wiped his hands with an oily rag.

"I'm going to have to order a new crankshaft," he said.

"And how long will that take?" demanded Mr Prenderghast.

Mr Montague sucked air through his teeth. "Normally you'll be looking at Friday at the earliest. But for a good client like yourself, I reckon I can get one for Tuesday."

Mr Prenderghast nodded. "Excellent."

Maud noticed that Penelope was staring at them from one of the upstairs rooms. She was starting to feel a little sorry for the witch. It had to be really frustrating to stay in a house with such lovely grounds but be forbidden from playing in them.

"I suppose I ought to invite you along to my party tonight," said Mr Prenderghast. "I've recently renovated a run-down property in the town square, and tonight I'll be opening it as a five-star hotel. It's amazing what I do for this town."

"It's nice of you to offer," said Mr Montague. "But we've got the girls to look after."

"You can bring them along too," said Mr Prenderghast, taking a wad of black invitations from his jacket.

"Monstrous!" said Maud. She grabbed the invitations and grinned up at Penelope, who was scowling from the window.

As her dad drove her home, Maud examined the invitations, frowning.

"It says the party is at the Old Theatre," said Maud. "I can't believe Mr Prenderghast has turned the town's only theatre into a boring hotel."

"I suppose there must be more money in five-star service and champagne bars than the arts," said Mr Montague. "It's a real shame, though. Your mum will be heartbroken. She has loads of friends in the theatre group, and she's been designing costumes for them since before you and your sister were born."

As they pulled into the driveway of their house, a rotten smell wafted into the car.

"That rat of yours hasn't been at the bins again, has he?" asked Mr Montague.

"No," said Maud. "He only eats crisps and snacks these days."

The smell got stronger as they opened the front door. It reminded Maud of the time she left a banana in her locker at Primrose Towers over the Easter holidays.

Maud followed the smell into the kitchen, where Milly was crushing fruits and flowers with a rolling pin. On the table there was a row of empty glass bottles and a sheet of stickers with '*Special* by Milly Montague' written on them in curly purple letters.

"That's your perfume?" asked Maud. "Aren't perfumes supposed to smell good?"

"Very funny," snorted Milly. "If you must know, I just haven't got the mixture right yet. It's going to smell of summer meadows and unicorns when it's finished."

Unicorn droppings maybe, thought Maud. She retreated to the living room, trying not to breathe in too much. Dad was showing the party invites to her mum, who was frowning.

"We don't have to go," said Mr Montague. "I know it might be hard for you."

"My lovely theatre," muttered Mrs Montague, looking at the invite. "Oh well. It will be rude if we don't show our faces, at least. And it might be the last chance we get to visit the old place. It will be too expensive from now on."

Milly waltzed in from the kitchen holding one of the jars, full of clear liquid. "What was that about a party?"

"We're going to one tonight, treacle," said Mrs Montague. She tried to smile, but Maud could tell from her eyes that she was still sad.

"Yippee!" shouted Milly. "I can wear my pink princess dress and try out my new perfume!" She took the cork out of the bottle. "Anyone want to try it?"

Mr and Mrs Montague coughed as the smell hit their nostrils. Quentin peeked out of Maud's pocket, his nose twitching, and then his eyes closed and he sank back inside.

"Out of the way!" shouted Maud. She raced to the kitchen, grabbed a packet of prawn cocktail crisps and ran upstairs to revive her rat.

As she wafted the fishy snack under Quentin's nose, Maud thought about the inspection letter she'd seen in Penelope's drawer. The witch must have taken it. But something wasn't right, because if Penelope had been caught stealing the Head's post, she'd almost certainly have been expelled. What on earth could have made her take such a risk?

Chapter Five

aud straightened out her black dress as she walked up the wide steps in front of the building that was once the theatre.

Inside the foyer, men in dinner jackets and women in evening gowns were milling around while waiters poured champagne into their glasses and held out miniature food on silver platters.

Mr Prenderghast had replaced the ticket booth with a reception desk, but the theatre's plush red carpets and hanging chandeliers were still intact.

Maud noticed her mum wiping a tear from her eye as she looked at a corner of the room. The board showing pictures of previous productions had been ripped down and replaced with a banner reading:

HAVE A MAGICAL STAY

Mr Prenderghast wandered over to them, smiling widely. "So glad you could make it, Mr Monkton."

"It's Montague, actually."

"And I'm delighted that you came along too, Mary," he said to Maud, which made her sister giggle.

"I take it you're Mrs Monkton," he said, turning to Maud's mum.

"You've done a lovely job with the building," said Mrs Montague in an unsteady voice. "I used to come here all the time when it was the theatre."

Mr Prenderghast rolled his eyes. "And wasn't it just the most vulgar little place? You should have seen the amount of junk I had to get rid of. I had to hire five separate skips for all those silly plays, props and costumes. How they ever thought they could make any money from that sort of thing is beyond me."

"Some of us liked it," said Mrs Montague quietly to herself.

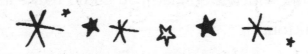

Maud could see her school friends beginning to arrive. Wilf's family had turned up wearing bulky hats and scarves to cover up their fur, and Warren was scooping pawfuls of canapés into his mouth, much to the disgust of the waiter.

"So you must have rather a lot of hotels now," said Mr Montague. "You're always popping up on the telly with all that 'Have a magical stay' business."

"Yes, this is my ninety-ninth hotel," said Mr Prenderghast. "Needless to say, the next one will be a very important milestone for me, and I have somewhere very special lined up …"

"Where's that?" asked Mr Montague.

"Now, now, Mr Monkfish," smiled Mr Prenderghast, tapping the side of his nose. "That would be telling."

Maud spotted Paprika entering with his parents Mr and Mrs Von Bat, so she pushed through the crowd to say hello. She thought there was a gap in the centre of the foyer, but when she shoved into it, she bumped into something instead.

"Hi, Maud," said the voice of Invisible Isabel.

"Oh, hi," said Maud. "I didn't see you arriving."

"Well, it is very crowded," said Isabel. "Anyway, let me introduce you to my mum,

Invisible Ingrid, and my dad, Invisible Ian."

"Lovely to meet you," said Maud, smiling at the empty space above her.

"Nice to meet you, too," said a deep voice.

"Hello, dear," said a woman's voice. "That's a very pretty dress you're wearing."

"Thanks," said Maud. "Yours is nice, too."

"But I'm wearing jeans," said the voice.

Maud cringed. "Of course you are, silly me. Well, I'd better be going."

Maud turned to see Milly staring at her with her hands on her hips. "I didn't realise you'd brought your imaginary friends," she said.

"Whatever," said Maud, ignoring her.

Paprika was trailing behind his mum, who was nagging his dad, but his face broke into a smile when he saw Maud approaching.

"Monstrous!" said Paprika. "I didn't know Penelope had invited you."

"She didn't actually invite me," said Maud. "But her Uncle Peregrine did."

"Good evening," said Mrs Von Bat. She was wearing a cream ballgown, decorated with white lace, and looked as if she'd strolled out of a costume drama. "We were just commenting on how much of an improvement all this is."

"Although the theatre was nice as well," added Mr Von Bat.

"Nonsense," said Mrs Von Bat. "It was just a lot of silly pretending."

Maud noticed Mr Von Bat blushing under his pale make-up. Although everyone at Rotwood thought he was a real vampire, she knew he was really just a human with plastic fangs and a cape.

"Let's sneak into the rest of the hotel," whispered Maud to Paprika. "Everyone's so busy chattering they won't notice."

Maud and Paprika found a door in one corner

of the foyer and snuck down the corridor that used to lead to the backstage area of the theatre.

She'd visited the theatre just a few weeks ago to watch a production of *Dracula*, and the corridor had been damp and bare, with brick walls and a dusty floor. Now it had thick red carpets and mirrored walls with the 'PP' logo etched on them.

"I went around to Mr Prenderghast's house today," said Maud. "Dad had to fix one of his cars."

"I bet it was monstrous," said Paprika. "He's got stacks of cash."

"It was pretty cool," said Maud. "But there's something really strange about him. And Penelope was being even weirder than usual, too. I saw a letter in her room that I think was meant for the Head. I'm pretty sure it was a warning about the inspection."

Paprika gasped. "And Penelope stole it?"

"I think so," said Maud.

"Imagine if the Head found out," said Paprika. "Penelope would pretty much have to move into the detention dungeon for good."

The door flew open, and Penelope came in and scowled at them.

"I might have known you two party poopers would be skulking around somewhere," said Penelope. "Anyway, you need to come back to the entrance hall. It's time to toast my uncle for being such an extremely brilliant man."

Chapter Six

$\mathcal{M}$aud was trying to concentrate on her textbook, but the class was too noisy and had collapsed into chaos.

There was a swoosh of wind in the corridor outside, and the Head flew in through the closed door. Everyone darted back to their seats and faced the front.

"I'm afraid there's bad news," said the Head. "Mr Von Bat is off ill today. He has food poisoning."

"Must have been the nibbles at the party," said Paprika.

"Well, my brother ate loads, and he's fine," said Wilf. "But that's werewolves for you. He ate a tennis ball once."

"There was nothing wrong with the food at my uncle's hotel," said Penelope. "Those vol-au-vents were absolutely first class."

"Anyway, the good news is that I've arranged for a supply teacher called Mrs Curmudgeon to come in," said the Head.

The door was flung aside, and a large woman with a long pale face, curly red hair and a ragged floral dress stomped in. She had smudgy red lipstick and blue eye shadow caked on.

"Let me know if you have any problems with this lot," said the Head.

"I doubt they'll give me much to worry about," boomed Mrs Curmudgeon in a deep voice.

"Very well," said the Head, and floated out through the door.

"What sort of a monster do you think she

is?" whispered Paprika. "A troll? An ogre? A stunted giant?"

"Shush!" shouted Mrs Curmudgeon, banging her meaty fist on the desk. "Now I've heard about your inspection last week, and let me tell you, there won't be any trouble on my watch. By the time I'm finished with you lot, Rotwood will be able to pass for a human school like Primrose Towers."

"Ewww," said Wilf. "Dad drove us past Primrose Towers last week, and it made my fur stand on end."

Several pupils tittered, but Mrs Curmudgeon scowled at Wilf, with her cheeks flushing red.

There was something very odd about the teacher, but Maud couldn't work out what it was. Then she noticed that her curls of red hair were moving. At first it seemed as though they were just twitching, but they soon began to writhe in and out of each other. Maud felt her stomach squirm as the curls formed tiny faces with black eyes and forked tongues.

"Of course," whispered Paprika. "She's a gorgon!"

The snakes on top of Mrs Curmudgeon's head turned to Wilf and hissed as one. Wilf sat bolt upright, and his skin started to turn grey. A strangled gasp escaped his mouth, and he went very still.

"Are you okay?" asked Billy Bones, who was sitting beside him.

Wilf didn't move an inch. Billy Bones reached over and gave him a firm tap. It sounded as if he was rapping his knuckles on stone.

"He's a statue!" gasped Billy.

"Is he dead, Miss?" asked Paprika, looking worried.

"Of course not," said Mrs Curmudgeon. "He'll be perfectly alright in about an hour.

He's merely petrified."

"He's not the only one," whispered Paprika.

"But let it be a lesson to the rest of you," said Mrs Curmudgeon. "I'm quite prepared to turn the whole classroom into a sculpture park if that's what it takes to make you behave."

Maud never would have believed that she'd be missing Mr Von Bat after just ten minutes.

"Now the first thing we need to sort out is the warning drill," said Mrs Curmudgeon. "I need a volunteer to keep watch at the school gates for the Inspector's return."

"Penelope can do it," said Isabel. 'She could fly back on her broom and warn us."

Mrs Curmudgeon glanced over at Penelope and then shook her head. "No, that's not going to work." She pointed at Paprika. "You, vampire boy, can you turn into a bat?"

"Yes, Miss," said Paprika.

"You'll do, then." Mrs Curmudgeon stamped across to the window and looked out. Heavy rain lashed against the glass. "Right, how fast can you get there and back?"

She took a stopwatch out of her pocket and glared at Paprika.

"What, right now?" asked Paprika. "In the pouring rain?"

"Yes, in the pouring rain," said Mrs Curmudgeon. Her hair was starting to twitch. "You – the zombie boy – open the window."

Paprika's eyes widened. He pelted towards the window and launched himself out of it just as Zak pushed it open. A puff of smoke enveloped him, and he flew out of it as a small black bat.

"Go!" shouted Mrs Curmudgeon, clicking her stopwatch. She turned back to the class. "The rest of you are to make your way down to the entrance hall. Mr Quasimodo will be waiting for you with cleaning and painting materials."

Mrs Curmudgeon went around the room and assigned mopping, dusting and painting roles to the pupils. When she got to Maud, she smiled wickedly. "You can scrub the floors," she said. But when she passed Penelope, she said nothing at all.

"Miss, why hasn't Penelope been given a job?" asked Zak.

Mrs Curmudgeon considered this for a minute. "We're going to need an overseer. That can be Penelope's role."

"Does that mean I'm the boss?" asked Penelope.

"That's right," said Mrs Curmudgeon.

✳ ★ ✳ ☆ ★ ✳

Penelope stretched her hands behind her head and put her feet up on the desk.

Maud heard a cracking noise from the front of the class. Wilf was moving, and flakes of stone crumbled from his fur. He shook himself. "What happened?" he said.

"You just got assigned scrubbing duty," said Mrs Curmudgeon.

As Maud stood up to leave the room, she spotted Paprika flying back towards the open window. Penelope must have noticed, too, because she wiggled her fingers at the window and whispered under her breath. It slammed shut, and Paprika banged into it over and over again with a look of frustration on his tiny bat face.

"We're supposed to be working together," said Maud. She rushed over to the window to let Paprika in.

There was a puff of smoke, and Paprika collapsed on to the floor, drenched and gasping with exhaustion.

Mrs Curmudgeon clicked her stopwatch. "Three minutes and forty-one seconds. That's pathetic, bat boy. You're going to have to do better. Off you go again."

"What? Right now?" asked Paprika.

"Are you disobeying me?" said Mrs Curmudgeon.

Paprika pulled himself off the floor and climbed up on to the windowsill. "I can't wait for Dad to get better," he muttered, and launched himself off once more.

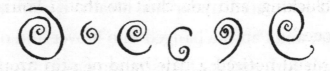

Maud dipped the wooden brush in the bucket of dirty water and tried again. She'd been scrubbing the flagstones of the entrance hall for over an hour and all she'd managed to uncover was fresh layers of dirt.

Maud leant on the brush and wiped her forehead with her sleeve.

"This is no time for slacking," said Mrs Curmudgeon from the back of the hall.

"This is no time for slacking," Wilf repeated in a silly voice. He was working on the stone next to Maud.

"I heard that," said Mrs Curmudgeon, pacing towards the werewolf. The curls of her hair started knotting in and out of each other again, and Wilf cringed behind his hands.

"Luckily for you," said Mrs Curmudgeon, pointing a stubby finger, "I need the drains unblocking, and you can't do that if you're a statue."

Maud noticed a pale band of skin around the teacher's index finger. It was like the mark she saw on her mum's finger when she took her wedding ring off to do the washing up.

Something rang a bell in the back of Maud's mind. Something else about a ring ...

✳ ✦ ✳ ✩ ★ ✳

After morning break, the class went out to the playing field to practise putting on their disguises as quickly as possible. Although Maud didn't really need one, she thought she'd better join in by putting her jacket on as fast as she could.

The pupils lined up in a neat row with piles of hats, coats and scarves in front of them, while the PE teacher Mr Galahad rode up and down on his giant stag beetle.

"Now, troops, you'll have ten seconds to whip on your disguises after I blow the whistle," he said. "Is that clear?"

"Yes, Sir," chanted the class.

"Righty-ho," said Mr Galahad. He tooted his whistle, and everyone lunged for their coats and scarves.

Maud slipped on her jacket with ease and watched the rest of the class struggle. All along the line, pupils were fumbling with sleeves and bashing each other with stray limbs.

The whistle blew again, and Mr Galahad inspected the pupils. Martin the mummy had somehow managed to get his zip tangled in his bandages. Oscar's head had fallen off and rolled across the field. And Roger the demon had put his baseball cap on so fast that he'd impaled it on one of his horns.

"What a mess!" shouted Mr Galahad, his cheeks flushing purple. "No good at all!"

By lunchtime, Maud was exhausted but had no appetite to eat her sandwich. She perched on a bench in the dingy lunch hall and fed Quentin the cheese from it. Next to her, Zombie Zak had slumped forward and fallen asleep in his brain stew. Maud had never seen him so tired. He could usually potter around saying "Ug" all day without a rest.

Paprika and Wilf plonked themselves down on the bench opposite Maud. Paprika's cape was dripping puddles on to the floor. He sneezed loudly. "I think I'm getting a cold."

"She's got to be stopped," said Wilf, glancing over his shoulder in case Mrs Curmudgeon was listening in again. "It's an abuse of our monster rights."

"I happen to think she's doing a wonderful job," butted in Penelope from the bench behind Wilf. "It's about time someone instilled some discipline around here. In fact, I'm going to suggest that the Head makes her a permanent member of staff."

Wilf howled at the top of his voice, and Paprika put his head in his hands.

"Maybe someone should go to the Head and complain," said Invisible Isabel.

Wilf and Paprika turned to look at Maud expectantly.

"I know you can't see me, but I'm looking at you, too," said Isabel.

"Why me?" asked Maud.

"Well," said Paprika, "you *are* Head Girl."

Chapter Seven

Maud tiptoed among the black cats that were prowling the floor of the Head's office and took a seat.

"What can I do for you, Montague?" asked the Head.

"It's about Mrs Curmudgeon," said Maud.

"Oh yes? She seems to have everything in hand."

Maud didn't know where to look, so she stared at her feet. "Some pupils think she's a little on the strict side," she said. "Everyone's exhausted, and Mrs Curmudgeon cut lunch break short to get on with the redecoration."

"I'm sorry to hear that," said the Head. "But she's right to be anxious. I'm really beginning to wonder if the days of this school are numbered."

"No!" said Maud.

The Head floated over to her window and looked out on to a landscape of wonky, rain-lashed graves. "Perhaps I was foolish to think this place could go on for ever. It was only a matter of time before a human Inspector turned up for a surprise visit."

Maud wanted to tell the Head about the letter she'd seen in Penelope's desk, but she needed to work out what the witch was up to first. Besides, she couldn't just accuse her of stealing the letter. She needed proof.

"I just felt there ought to be a place where monsters could learn and grow without being treated as outcasts," said the Head.

Maud thought back to her old school, Primrose Towers, and realised that the Head was right. They used to think she was a freak just because she had a pet rat and a bug collection. She couldn't imagine how they'd have reacted if she'd turned invisible or removed her head.

"Then when I saw this building, I knew I'd found the place," continued the Head. "I didn't think anyone else would want to buy a derelict building in the middle of a bog, but there was a man at the auction who seemed to be just as keen on it as me. I ended up spending all the money I'd saved when I was alive, on this place. If it gets shut down, I'll have nowhere to go."

"We won't let that happen!" said Maud.

✳ ★ ✳ ☆ ★ ✳

Instead of taking them for Fright Class that afternoon, Mrs Curmudgeon led Class 3B down to the assembly hall, where Mr Fortissimo was playing Bach's Toccata and Fugue in D Minor.

"Play the signal," ordered Mrs Curmudgeon.

Mr Fortissimo cracked his fingers and started to play Chopsticks instead. As he did so, a wooden panel in the wall at the back of the hall swished aside to reveal a set of stone steps spiralling down into murky gloom.

"This is the secret storeroom," said Mrs Curmudgeon. "All supernatural items must be placed inside until after the inspection. That means every coffin, cauldron, crystal ball, spare leg, jar of eyeballs, giant stag beetle, bottle of blood, box of curried brains, pickled worms and spider soufflé. Is that clear?"

Billy Bones swiped Oscar's head off his shoulders, and held it up. "Miss, does this count as a supernatural item?"

"Don't be ridiculous," said Mrs Curmudgeon. "He needs that for his homework."

Oscar snatched his head back.

"But what about Penelope's broomstick?" asked Wilf. "Should we put that in there?"

"No," said Mrs Curmudgeon. "She's smart

enough to keep it out of sight. Now get moving! Fetch all your magical items right now!"

As the pupils marched out of the hall, Maud hung back to look at Mrs Curmudgeon. There was something very strange about the lumbering teacher that she couldn't quite put her finger on. Why was she giving Penelope so much preferential treatment?

Mrs Curmudgeon spotted Maud and pointed at her. "I said get a move on! I won't tell you again. I knew you were a trouble-maker!"

The red curls of Mrs Curmudgeon's hair began to snake around each other, and Maud felt her skin tighten.

"Yes, Miss," said Maud. As she backed away towards the door, she noticed the pale mark of the ring on her teacher's pointing finger once more. It was as if a light bulb switched on in her head. Hadn't Igor, Peregrine's doorman, been wearing a signet ring in that exact place? Was it possible ...

Maud peered closer at Mrs Curmudgeon. She certainly was tall, and her voice was rather deep.

And Maud had never seen Igor without a hat on. Perhaps it had been hiding a mess of snakes all along. It also explained why the supply teacher was always so nice to Penelope.

Maud swallowed. It seemed so obvious now.

Mrs Curmudgeon and Igor were the same person!

As soon as the last lesson of the day was over, Maud dashed to the first floor and opened the door of the library. Inside, she could see hundreds of rows of uneven shelves still caked in dust. In the middle of the room was a row of desks with flickering candles, and at the back a man was packing books into cardboard boxes.

"How now?" he asked. He had long, thinning

hair with a straggly moustache and a stiff white ruff around his neck. The man walked over to Maud and shook her hand. He was wearing a doublet and hose. "Good morrow. I'm Mr Shakespeare, the librarian."

"I'm looking for a book on monsters," said Maud.

"We have many," said the man. "But alas, I've been ordered to ship them all down to the secret storeroom."

"You've probably heard this before," said Maud, "but you look just like the real Shakespeare. Are you related?"

The librarian frowned. "I *am* the real Shakespeare."

"I thought you died four hundred years ago," said Maud.

"Perhaps," said Mr Shakespeare. "But I remain on this great stage."

Maud nodded. "Well, if you're the real Shakespeare, why are you working as a school librarian? Surely you can use your writing skills to make a living?"

"Zounds!" said Mr Shakespeare. "I submit things to publishers all the time, but they prefer memoirs of reality TV stars these days. A pox on them! But anon, what manner of beast did you want to read about?"

"Gorgons," said Maud. "I need to find out if they can be male as well as female. It's er … for my school project."

Mr Shakespeare delved into one of the boxes and pulled out a book called *Legendary Bestiary*. He scanned through. "Gorgons … gorgons … It says the most famous was Medusa, who got her head chopped off by Perseus. He used a mirror to see her, so he didn't have to look at her horrible image. It says that male gorgons exist, but are extremely rare, and not as powerful as the female variety. In fact, they can only turn victims to stone for a few minutes at a time."

Maud thought of Wilf becoming a statue

until the end of the lesson.

"Monstrous!" she said, "I've got a mirror at home. Thanks for helping!"

"As you like it," said Mr Shakespeare, returning to his packing.

Maud looked at the Monsters and Magic section of the library, which was now completely bare. "Won't those empty shelves make the Inspector suspicious?"

"Nay. We're going to fill them with these books from the Horror section," said Mr Shakespeare. He pointed to a pile of books with pink, sparkly covers. Maud was puzzled for a moment and then she remembered – monsters are terrified of anything pink and fluffy. There was *Pink Princess Party, Ickle Puppy Adventures* and *Fairy Frilly's Magic Cottage*.

"My sister loves those books," said Maud.

As Maud passed through the entrance hall, she saw that the pupils on painting duty were still slaving away under the careful watch of

Mrs Curmudgeon. Billy Bones had pink paint all over himself. He'd need a good bleaching when he got home.

Maud made straight for the main exit in case the teacher spotted her and decided that the floor needed an extra scrub.

As she climbed on to the school bus, Maud wondered about what Mr Shakespeare had said. She was sure that Igor and Mrs Curmudgeon were the same person, and that meant that Mr Prenderghast was up to something. But what?

$$* \quad * * \quad * \quad * \quad *$$

As the bus pulled up and the doors opened at Maud's stop, a strange, rotten scent wafted in. Several pupils pulled their jackets up over their noses.

Maud stepped towards her house, where the foul smell got even stronger. She wondered if the drains were blocked. Or maybe someone's toilet had exploded. Then she saw that the garage door was wide open, and Milly was inside crushing bananas with a hammer, and draining the juice into her perfume bottles.

"That would certainly get you noticed at parties," said Maud.

"Shut up, Maud," said Milly. "It just needs a couple of tweaks."

A couple of tweaks, and it would be suitable for chemical warfare, thought Maud. She was just about to open the front door when her dad dashed out, frantically pulling his driving gloves on.

"Hello, cupcake," he said. "I've got to dash over to Mr Prenderghast's house. The limousine part has just been delivered."

"I'll come!" said Maud. It sounded like another good chance to investigate what Penelope's uncle was up to. Plus, it would get her away from the smell of Milly's perfume. "I, er, need to borrow a schoolbook from Penelope."

"Hop in, then," said Mr Montague. "It's very sweet that you want to see your little friend." Maud nodded, although there was nothing sweet about it really. She had to find out what Mr Prenderghast was plotting – and fast.

Chapter Eight

The door to Mr Prenderghast's mansion swung open.

"Welcome back," boomed Igor.

Maud tried to get a good look at him as she passed. Could he really have got back and changed so quickly? There was no sign of movement under his hat, but she was convinced there was a tiny smudge of lipstick at the side of his mouth.

"I'll go straight up and see Penelope, if that's okay," she said.

"Very well," said Igor. Maud hoped he'd

disappear back into the house so she could snoop around, but he stood and watched her as she walked up the stairs to the second floor corridor.

Maud turned into it and scanned around for clues. There was a photo of Penelope and her uncle riding their broomsticks on a flying holiday to Transylvania. They were swooping past the ruin of an old castle and waving at the camera. There was also a photo of Penelope with a man who must have been her dad. He had a long blue cape and purple hair that was thinning on top. He was wearing a T-shirt that said, "I've met Merlin and he taught me everything he knows." Next to this was a certificate from the WWWF – the Wicked Witches and Warlocks Foundation – thanking Mr Prenderghast for his kind donation of one hundred cauldrons to help underprivileged young sorcerers.

None of this was helping her. She had to get into Mr Prenderghast's private rooms if she was to have any hope of learning his plans. She could bet her eyeballs that the evidence she needed was hidden in the study – the one Igor had got so cross with her for going into last time.

Maud knocked on Penelope's door and went inside. Penelope was perched on the edge of her bed, brushing her long purple hair. She looked up at Maud and frowned.

"You again?" she asked. "Did someone tell you I wanted to be your best friend forever or something? Because if they did, they were lying."

"I'm just here with Dad again," said Maud. "I wouldn't have come up at all, but I saw Igor raking up leaves with your broomstick in the garden, and I thought you'd want to know."

"What?" asked Penelope. She dashed over to the door, turned and shouted back, "Touch anything while I'm gone and I'll turn your hands into frogs!"

"I won't," said Maud, with her fingers crossed.

As soon as she heard Penelope's footsteps on the stairs, Maud dashed over to the desk and pulled open the top drawer. There were a few spell books and a membership card for the Society of Young Witches, but there was no sign of the letter.

"Drat!" said Maud. She searched on top of the table, lifting up a jar of lizard tongues, a packet of dried beetles and a bottle of invisibility potion, but the letter wasn't there either.

Maud recognised Igor's deep, booming voice coming from the room below. She lifted up the corner of Penelope's rug and put her ear to the wooden floorboards.

"Is there anything else you require?" thundered Igor.

"We just need to hold our nerve," replied Mr Prenderghast in a softer voice. "Our plan is almost complete."

Maud grabbed the invisibility potion from Penelope's desk and splashed it over the floor. The liquid seeped around the wooden boards and down on to the plaster of ceiling below, until Maud could peer all the way down into Mr Prenderghast's study.

The sheet had been removed from the table in the middle to reveal a model of a building. It took Maud only a few seconds to realise it was Rotwood School. She'd seen it from the air before, when Penelope once grudgingly gave her a lift home on her broomstick.

The grounds surrounding the school looked very different from the current ones, however. Instead of the graveyard to one side, there was a terraced dining area with parasols and outdoor heaters. The playing fields at the back had been replaced by tennis courts. And instead of the spooky forest, there was a golf driving range.

Maud felt her heart quicken. So that was Prenderghast's wicked plan! Rotwood would be his hundredth development. After all the work her great-aunt Ethel had put into the school, that wicked wizard was planning to convert it into a hotel!

"That Montague child is becoming a little too suspicious," grumbled Igor from below.

Mr Prenderghast scoffed out a laugh. "What if she is? There's nothing she can do. Rotwood will fail its inspection, and the building will be mine at long last."

Maud heard Penelope stomping upstairs again, and she flopped the rug back into place over the spilt potion.

$$\maltese \quad \star \quad \maltese \quad \star \quad \bigstar \quad \maltese$$

Penelope came in, clutching her broom. "This was propped up against the garage wall where I left it. And I couldn't see Igor anywhere. Is this your idea of a joke? Are you up to something?"

"Oh," said Maud. "Then I was mistaken."

Penelope folded her arms and glared at her.

"Alright then," said Maud. "I am up to something. I'm trying to stop your greedy uncle from shutting down Rotwood School."

Penelope rolled her eyes. "Don't be ridiculous."

"Stop pretending you don't know what I'm talking about," said Maud. "I saw that inspection letter to the Head in your drawer, and I know that Mrs Curmudgeon is actually Igor."

Penelope stared at Maud in silence for a minute and then shrugged. "Well, maybe my uncle *should* take over Rotwood. I'm sure he'd do a better job than that dreary old ghost who runs it at the moment."

"How can you say that about the Head?" asked Maud. "She's always trying to do the best thing for all the pupils. Including you!"

"She's past it," said Penelope. "When my uncle's in charge, he's going to push the school to new levels of excellence. There'll be better books, better equipment, better teachers …"

"There'll be none of those things," cried Maud, "because there won't *be* a school at all. Your wonderful uncle is planning to turn Rotwood into a hotel!"

"He can't be," said Penelope, her voice wavering slightly. "That's not what he said."

"I'll prove it to you," said Maud. She pulled back the rug and pointed through the invisible potion to the model.

Penelope peered down through the floor, and gasped. "But he told me it would be the greatest monster school in the world. He said I'd be Head Prefect. He said I could give detentions whenever I pleased."

"Your uncle has probably made a lot of promises he hasn't kept over the years," said Maud.

"I don't believe it," said Penelope.

"We'll all be transferred to Primrose Towers," said Maud. "You'll get picked on every day for having purple hair."

Penelope glanced in the mirror above her desk. "But my purple hair is pretty."

"It might be to you," said Maud. "But try convincing those Primrose Towers girls. You'll get torn apart!"

"Alright, alright, I get it," said Penelope. "But how can we stop him?"

"I don't know," said Maud. "I think your uncle and Igor are planning something for the inspection, but I don't know what. We need to stay on the alert. If the inspection goes wrong, it'll mean the end of Rotwood!"

Chapter Nine

Milly thrust a bottle of her perfume into Maud's face in the kitchen the next morning.

"Ta-dah!" she shouted. "It's perfect. Finally! Try some, stinkums."

"No thanks," said Maud, chomping on a piece of toast. The truth was, she would rather have coated herself in frogspawn.

"Well, at least put some on your rancid rat," said Milly, unscrewing the top.

Quentin, who was eating his breakfast, leapt into Maud's jacket pocket.

"I'll take some for later," said Maud, grabbing the bottle from Milly. She had no intention of inflicting that stink on Quentin, but at least it would stop her sister from unleashing the perfume while she was eating.

Maud glanced down at her watch and saw that she only had five minutes until the school bus came. She darted to the door, then remembered something. She ran back inside to fetch her mum's hand mirror from her dressing table. She knew it would come in handy today with a gorgon teacher on the rampage.

When Maud got to school she was alarmed to see that the entrance hall was now completely pink. The dripping candles had been replaced by bright electric lights, and the windows were so clean you could actually see through them. Above one of the doors to the left, was a framed picture of a kitten, and above a corridor on the right, there was a bad painting of a rainbow.

Maud noticed Mr Von Bat at the side of the hall and ran over to him.

"Glad to see you're better, Sir," she said.

"I'm afraid Mrs Curmudgeon is still teaching though," said Mr Von Bat. "She'll be taking Class 3B this morning. I'm not feeling up to it quite yet."

Maud continued through to the assembly hall and sat down on one of the pews. Usually, the hall echoed with chattering, screaming and barking before the Head arrived, but this morning everyone was slumped forward, looking dejected.

The Head emerged from the wall and floated over to her lectern.

"Morning monsters," said the Head. "I want to tell you all what a super job you've done. I can honestly say I've never seen Rotwood looking so bright and clean. I'm now confident that whenever the inspection happens, we'll pass with flying colours."

Maud couldn't bear to see the Head so full of hope, while Mr Prenderghast and his gorgon side-kick were plotting against her. She had to tell her, and she had to tell her now. She stuck her hand in the air. Mrs Curmudgeon looked over, with her curls quivering.

"Not now, Montague," said the Head. "So, I know some of you have been complaining that the kitten picture has given you a headache, but I can assure you I'll take it down as soon as the inspection is over."

"Miss!" shouted Maud. She didn't care if she ended up getting turned to stone. She had to let the Head know there was something going on.

"What is it, Montague?" asked the Head.

Maud was about to speak, when a bat swooped into the hall. There was a puff of smoke, and Paprika fell out of it and rolled across the floor, his arms flailing about. He came to a halt in front of the lectern and jumped to his feet.

"He's here!" he cried. "The Inspector's here!"

The hall filled with gasps and anxious murmurs.

"Nobody panic," said the Head. "Just follow the drill."

There was a scrum of arms, legs and tails, as the pupils pulled their disguises on. Warren put his coat on back to front and yelped with confusion, and Billy Bones got his scarf tangled in his vertebrae, but on the whole the pupils managed fairly well.

Next to Maud, Mr Von Bat put in a set of large fake teeth to cover his fake fangs and removed his black cape to reveal a brown suit.

"You look almost like an ordinary human now," said Maud, smiling.

"Watch it, Montague," said Mr Von Bat. "When this is over, everything will be back to how it was. And I won't be above giving out detentions for cheek."

"Alright, monsters," said the Head. "Or should I say, humans. Go back to your classrooms and act as normally as you can."

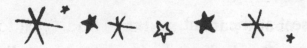

Maud climbed up the spiral staircase to her classroom. Through the narrow window halfway up, she saw a man with neat hair in a suit, jotting down notes on his clipboard. His eyes were darting around nervously, and Maud wondered if he'd heard what had happened to the last Inspector.

Penelope stomped up to Maud as she was approaching the classroom. "Thanks for stealing my invisibility potion."

"I didn't touch it," said Maud.

"Well, someone has," said Penelope. She lifted the flap of her satchel to reveal a row of small bottles of clear liquid and pointed to a gap in the middle.

"Sit down," growled Mrs Curmudgeon, taking her seat at the front.

The Head floated through the wall and swooped around the class, making sure everything was in order.

"Miss, can I tell you something?" said Maud, but the Head took no notice.

"Good, good," said the Head. "Now if we can just make it through the next hour or so, our future will be secure."

"Miss!" shouted Maud again. "Wait!"

But the Head zipped towards the wall and disappeared through it.

"There are three main types of rock …" droned Mrs Curmudgeon from the front of the class. The Inspector had been in the school for almost half an hour now, and things seemed to be going well as far as Maud could tell.

She hadn't heard any cries of horror, and Mrs Curmudgeon had been in front of her the whole time, apparently behaving herself. Everything monstrous was safely stored beneath the main hall.

"I think we might get away with this," whispered Wilf, "unless the Inspector can see through floors."

Maud felt as though her heart had stopped.

"Of course!" she said. "That's it!"

Wilf looked puzzled.

Maud leaned over to Penelope and hissed, "I know where your bottle is. It's in her bag." She pointed to Mrs Curmudgeon's black handbag, which was perched on the edge of the desk.

"You mean *his* bag," said Penelope.

"He's going to pour it all over the floor of the assembly hall and reveal the supernatural stash in the room below. We need to stop him!"

"Stop that wittering," said Mrs Curmudgeon from the front of the room. "It might have escaped your attention, but we have an inspection going on right now."

"Sorry," said Maud. "I was asking Penelope if she knew what a sedimentary rock was."

"You'll find out, if you don't shut up," said Mrs Curmudgeon. "Because I'll turn you into one."

As the teacher warbled on about rocks again, Maud stared at the handbag, wondering how to snatch the potion without getting caught.

There was a rustling inside Maud's pocket. Quentin peeped up at her.

"It's not crisp time yet," whispered Maud. She looked at Quentin, and an idea occurred to her. "Though I might make an exception today."

She pointed at Mrs Curmudgeon's handbag, and Quentin looked over at it, his nose twitching. "Potion," she hissed. "Do you understand, Quentin? Potion."

Quentin nodded, leapt out of her pocket and landed gracefully on the floor.

Maud turned to Penelope and whispered, "I need a distraction! Quick!"

Penelope wiggled her fingers at the door and muttered under her breath until a loud knock sounded.

Mrs Curmudgeon broke off from her lecture about rocks and looked at the door. "Come in."

There was no reply. The supply teacher sighed and pulled herself up from her chair. She opened the door on to the empty corridor.

"Is that you, Isabel?" asked Mrs Curmudgeon.

"Of course not, Miss," said Isabel. "I've been sitting next to your desk for the last half hour."

Maud's eyes were on Quentin, who'd just undone the clasp of the handbag with his teeth. He needed an extra couple of seconds.

"I think I heard someone run off down the corridor," said Maud. "Maybe they're playing a prank on you."

Mrs Curmudgeon stuck her head out of the door and looked around. "Well, they've gone now," she said, slamming the door. She tramped back to her desk and plonked herself down again as Quentin darted across the floor, clutching something in his paws. Maud held her breath, hoping he hadn't brought hand lotion by mistake. But no – Quentin placed a small bottle at Maud's feet. Penelope's potion!

"Clever boy," she said, handing him a crisp. "But if you want another one, you're going to have to brave the handbag again. Do you understand?"

Quentin looked at Maud and squeaked.

"Excellent," said Maud.

Chapter Ten

It was morning break, and Maud, Paprika and Penelope had snuck into the assembly hall to watch the Inspector chat to the Head and Mr Von Bat. The Head was doing an excellent job of pretending to stand on the floor, even though she normally floated a few centimetres above it.

"Well, this seems to be in order," he said.

"I'm so glad you think so," said the Head.

"I'm going to recommend the school for an outstanding performance certificate," said the Inspector. He nodded to the Head. "Keep up the good work," he said.

"Monstrous!" said Paprika, peering over the pew they were hiding behind. "We passed!"

"I don't think it's over just yet," said Maud. She pointed to the side of the hall, where Mrs Curmudgeon was striding towards the Inspector. The gorgon teacher stood in front of him, blocking his path.

"I think there's one last thing you should see before you leave," she said.

She unzipped her handbag and took out a small bottle.

"Take a look at this," she said, triumphantly.

Maud held her breath as Mrs Curmudgeon popped the cork off and poured clear liquid across the floor.

Immediately, the air was filled with the delicate scent of peaches and rosebuds. The Head and Mrs Curmudgeon wafted their hands in front of their faces.

Penelope held her nose and spluttered, while

Paprika coughed and wiped tears from his eyes.

"What on earth is that?" he asked.

"That's *Special*, by Milly Montague," said Maud. "And it smells as if she finally managed to get it right."

"Just wait a minute," said Mrs Curmudgeon, shaking the last drops from the bottle. "I think it takes a couple of moments to kick in."

"Not at all," said the Inspector. "I can smell it right now, and it's glorious. In fact, I'm going to give you an extra mark for the lovely thought."

"Well, thanks again for coming," said Mr Von Bat, hastily leading the Inspector back to the entrance hall.

The Head hurried after them, still pretending to walk, even though she normally drifted.

"We do try to make our guests feel welcome," she said.

*⋆ ★ ✦ ☆ ★ ✳ ⋆

Maud and Penelope stood up from behind the pew and went over to Mrs Curmudgeon, who was scowling at the empty bottle.

"I got my rat to switch the invisibility potion for a bottle of stinky perfume," said Maud, "in case you were wondering."

Mrs Curmudgeon glared at Maud, the curls on her hair arching back and forth as if she was standing in a strong breeze.

"And that was my invisibility potion," said Penelope. "You should ask before you borrow things."

Mrs Curmudgeon was flushed a deep red now, her red hair twining into a slithering mass.

"How dare you speak to me like that? Don't you know who I am?"

"Yes," said Maud. The snakes on the gorgon's head had sprouted furious eyes and rasping tongues.

"You're a horrible gorgon doorman and you're a bully!"

The snakes drew their heads back as one, but as they did so, Maud reached into her bag and took out her mum's mirror. She shoved it at Mrs Curmudgeon and turned away.

Maud listened as the snakes hissed in unison, and Mrs Curmudgeon let out a groan, which cut off halfway through. When Maud looked back, she saw that the supply teacher had turned to stone, with a pained scowl on her face.

"And you need to learn to control your temper," Maud added.

Paprika stepped up to the frozen teacher and tapped her nose.

"That was so monstrous. It's a shame it's not permanent, really."

Maud heard loud engines grumbling to a halt outside.

"I don't think we're finished yet," she said.

They dashed out of the hall, down the corridor, through the entrance hall and out of the main exit.

Peregrine Prenderghast was standing outside the school wearing an expensive-looking suit and a hard hat, clutching a set of blueprints. To his right, was a large yellow digger with a sharp tilting claw. To his left, was a bulldozer with an enormous metal blade lowered. Workmen with hard hats, goggles and high-visibility jackets were sitting in the vehicles with their hands on the controls.

The Head, Mr Von Bat and the Inspector stared up at them from the side of the driveway.

Mr Prenderghast turned to the workmen and pointed to the side of the school. "We can start with the graveyard. I need it levelled for the dining terrace."

The workman in the digger turned his key in the ignition, but Mr Von Bat stepped out to block his path.

"What on earth are you doing to my school?" demanded the Head.

"I'm starting work on the renovation, of course," said Mr Prenderghast. He stared up at Rotwood with mad glee in his eyes. "The council gave me permission to buy this place if it failed its inspection. I intend to convert this mouldy old dump into Prenderghast Manor Luxury Hotel, and I don't want to waste a single second. So if you'd kindly move aside ..."

✳ ★ ✳ ✩ ★ ✳

"But the school didn't fail," said the Inspector. "This is an outstanding institution, and there's no way it should close."

"What? What about all the weird things beneath the assembly hall?" asked Mr Prenderghast. "All those cauldrons and coffins and monsters ..."

"I'm afraid I don't follow," said the Inspector.

"Perhaps you've got the wrong address."

"No, he hasn't," said the Head. "He's wanted to take this building from me since I beat him to it in that auction ten years ago. Isn't that true, Mr Prenderghast?"

"Forward!" shouted Mr Prenderghast. "On with the work!"

The workmen pushed their goggles up on to their foreheads and exchanged glances.

"I don't think we're allowed to," said the driver of the digger. "If the school passed its inspection, it would be more than my job's worth to go ahead with the work."

"Never mind the inspection!" shouted Mr Prenderghast, his eyes blazing. "The truth is that this is a monster school and it must be destroyed!"

The driver of the bulldozer folded his arms and stared at Mr Prenderghast. "Sorry, you've lost me. What's a 'monster school'?"

"It's a school for monsters, you silly peasant,"

ranted Mr Prenderghast. "Everyone here is a foul, supernatural beast."

"Don't be ridiculous," said the Head.

"You know I'm telling the truth, you daft old spook," said Mr Prenderghast. He glared at the workmen and the Inspector, who all looked away in embarrassment. "They're all wearing costumes and wigs. Watch …"

Mr Prenderghast ran up to Maud and tugged her hair.

"Owww," cried Maud. "That hurts!"

The driver of the digger stepped down from his cab and walked towards Mr Prenderghast. "I don't think you ought to be attacking little girls."

The bulldozer driver stepped down, too. "Maybe we ought to leave these poor teachers in peace."

"Yes, I think that would be a good idea," said Mr Von Bat.

Mr Prenderghast turned to Mr Von Bat, his forehead knotted with anger. "I know what you are! I've been warned about you! Well, get a load of this …" He pulled a crucifix and a clove of garlic out of his pocket and held them up to Mr Von Bat. "Begone, vampire!"

Mr Von Bat looked at the objects and shrugged. He turned to the workmen. "I think it would be better for everyone if you took him away."

The workmen nodded. They grabbed hold of Mr Prenderghast's arms and dragged him back to his car.

"You don't understand," shouted Mr Prenderghast.

"My niece is a witch, and she told me all about it! That woman over there is a ghost, and one of the pupils is invisible, and one of them is a skeleton …"

"It's a pity," said the Head. "Such a successful businessman … The pressure must have finally got to him."

✳ ✦ ✳ ✩ ★ ✳

That night, Maud sat around the dinner table with her mum and Milly. She was still grinning as she thought about how they'd beaten Mr Prenderghast.

"Nice day at school, petal?" asked Mrs Montague.

"You could say that," said Maud.

"Mine was rotten," said Milly. "Suzie Wentworth got an A plus for her perfume, and mine only got an A."

"I thought it was very nice," said Maud. Milly narrowed her eyes at her.

Just then, they heard the familiar chug of the family car pulling into their driveway. Five minutes later, their dad came in and peeled off his driving gloves.

"Evening dear," said Mrs Montague. "You're back early."

"I didn't expect to be," said Mr Montague. "I thought I'd have to do some more work on Mr Prenderghast's cars, but when I called round to his house, there was no reply. I was just about to give up, when his doorman came to the door looking very under the weather."

Maud's dad paused.

"It was really quite strange," he continued. "The man was really pale and had all this odd, flaky stuff on him. I could have sworn it was bits of stone."

"Stone?" said Maud innocently.

"Yes, so I asked what was going on, and he said that the whole job had been called off. It seems that old Prenderghast's taken a turn for the worse."

"That's a shame," said Mrs Montague. "Is he alright?"

"Not really," said Mr Montague. "Apparently he's been admitted to the Spooglewood Home for the Deranged."

Maud thought about the crazed look in Mr Prenderghast's eyes as he turned up to destroy her beloved school.

"I hope he has a magical stay," she muttered to herself.

Other titles by A. B. Saddlewick:

ISBN:
978-1-78055-072-5

ISBN:
978-1-78055-073-2

ISBN:
978-1-78055-074-9

EVEN MORE
Monstrous Maud
STORIES COMING SOON!

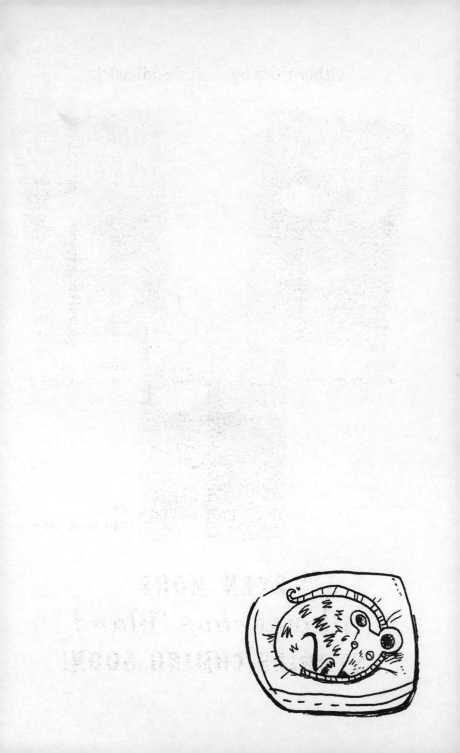